Paddington's Garden
Text copyright © 1972 by Michael Bond
Illustrations copyright © 1992 by HarperCollins Publishers Ltd.
First published in Great Britain by William Collins Sons and Co Ltd.
Printed and bound in Hong Kong
 All rights reserved.
2   3   4   5   6   7   8   9   10

First American Edition, 1993

Library of Congress Cataloging-in-Publication Data
Bond, Michael.
    Paddington's garden / Michael Bond ; illustrated by John
Lobban.—1st American ed.
        p.   cm.
    Summary: When he sets out to make his own rock garden in the
Brown's backyard, Paddington learns that gardening is hard work.
    ISBN 0-694-00462-6.
    [1. Bears—Fiction.   2. Gardening—Fiction.]   I. Lobban, John, ill.
II. Title.
PZ7.B6368Pak   1993   92-24527
[E]—dc20   CIP
                                                        AC

Paddington's Garden

Michael Bond

Illustrated by John Lobban

HarperFestival

A Division of HarperCollins*Publishers*

One day Paddington decided to make a list of all the nice things there were about being a bear and living with the Browns at number thirty-two Windsor Gardens.

It was a long list. When he had almost reached the bottom of the page, he realized that he'd forgotten one of the nicest things of all . . . the garden!

Paddington liked the Browns' garden. It was so quiet and peaceful there, it didn't seem like being in London at all.

But nice, big gardens require a lot of hard work, and after a day at the office, Mr. Brown often wished his garden wasn't quite so large.

It was Mrs. Brown who first thought of giving Jonathan, Judy, and Paddington their own little gardens.

"It will keep them out of trouble," she said.

"And they'll have fun at the same time."

So Mr. Brown measured out three squares. To make it more exciting, he said that he and Mrs. Brown would give a prize to whomever had the best idea.

Early the next morning, all three went to work.

Judy decided she would grow some flowers, and Jonathan wanted to make a paved garden, but Paddington didn't know what to do.

Gardening was much harder than it looked, and Paddington was getting very tired of digging.

So Paddington decided to take a break and go shopping.

He had some savings left over from his allowance, so he bought a wheelbarrow, a basket, a trowel, and a large package of assorted seeds.

It seemed like quite a bargain—he even had two pence left over.

The shopkeeper told him that when planning a new garden, it was helpful to look at the plot of land from a distance, and try to picture the finished garden. So, taking a jar of his best golden chunky marmalade, Paddington set out to visit the nearby building site.

By the time he got there it was the middle of the
morning. The workers were on their break, so Paddington
sat down on a pile of bricks, put the jar of marmalade on
a wooden platform where it would be safe, and looked
over at the Browns' garden.

BEST MARMALADE

After sitting there for some time without getting any ideas, Paddington decided to take a short walk.

When he got back, he couldn't believe his eyes.

A man was pouring cement on the very spot where he'd left his jar of golden chunky marmalade.

Just then, the foreman came around the corner. He saw the look on Paddington's face, and stopped to ask what was wrong.

Paddington pointed to the pile of wet cement.

"All my golden chunks have been buried!" he exclaimed.

The foreman called his workers together. "There's a young
bear gentleman here who's lost some very valuable golden
chunks," he said urgently.

They went to work clearing the cement.

Soon the ground was covered with small piles, but there was still no sign of Paddington's jar.

Suddenly they heard a whirring sound overhead. To Paddington's surprise, a platform landed at his feet.

"My marmalade!" he exclaimed thankfully.

"Your *marmalade*?" echoed the foreman, staring at the jar. "Did you say marmalade?"

"That's right," said Paddington. "I brought it along for my morning snack, and thought it would be safe on the platform."

It was the foreman's turn to look surprised.
"That's special quick-drying cement!" he yelled.
"It's probably rock-hard already—ruined by a
bear's marmalade!"

"No one will give me two pence for it now!"

Paddington opened his suitcase and felt around in the secret compartment. "*I* will," he said eagerly.

Paddington took the lumps of concrete home in his
wheelbarrow and worked hard in his garden for the rest
of the day. When the workers saw the rock garden he had
made with the cement, they were very impressed. They
gave Paddington several plants to finish it off until . . .

his own seeds started to grow.

Paddington's rock garden fit in so well with Jonathan's paved garden and Judy's flower bed that it looked as though all three gardens had been planned together.

Mr. and Mr. Brown were so pleased that they decided to give them all an extra week's allowance. That afternoon, everyone celebrated by having a picnic in the new garden.

Later, Paddington sat down to finish off his list of all the nice things there were about being a bear and living at number thirty-two Windsor Gardens.

He had one more important item to add.

MY ROCK GARDEN

Then he signed his name and added his special paw print . . .

. . . just to show that it was genuine.